PUFFIN BOOKS

# DIARY OF A WIMPY KID

# HARD LUCK

## BOOKS BY JEFF KINNEY

*Diary of a Wimpy Kid*

*Diary of a Wimpy Kid: Rodrick Rules*

*Diary of a Wimpy Kid: The Last Straw*

*Diary of a Wimpy Kid: Dog Days*

*Diary of a Wimpy Kid: The Ugly Truth*

*Diary of a Wimpy Kid: Cabin Fever*

*Diary of a Wimpy Kid: The Third Wheel*

*Diary of a Wimpy Kid: Hard Luck*

*The Wimpy Kid Do-It-Yourself Book*

*The Wimpy Kid Movie Diary*

COMING SOON

More *Diary of a Wimpy Kid*

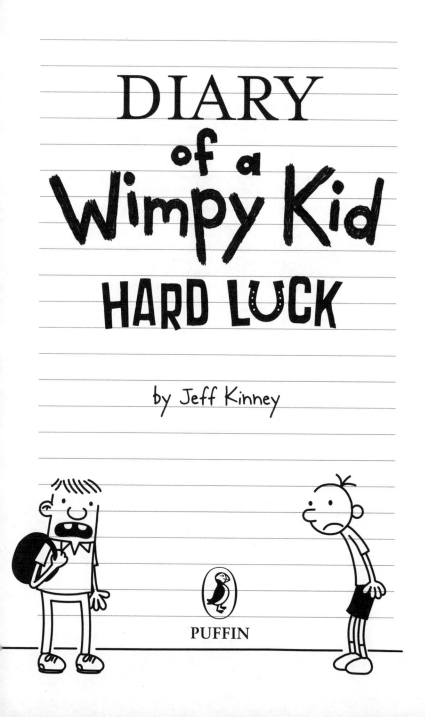

# DIARY
of a
# Wimpy Kid
# HARD LUCK

by Jeff Kinney

PUFFIN

PUFFIN BOOKS

Published by the Penguin Group
Penguin Books Ltd, 80 Strand, London WC2R ORL, England
Penguin Group (USA) Inc., 375 Hudson Street, New York, New York 10014, USA
Penguin Group (Canada), 90 Eglinton Avenue East, Suite 700, Toronto, Ontario, Canada M4P 2Y3
(a division of Pearson Penguin Canada Inc.)
Penguin Ireland, 25 St Stephen's Green, Dublin 2, Ireland (a division of Penguin Books Ltd)
Penguin Group (Australia), 707 Collins Street, Melbourne, Victoria 3008, Australia
(a division of Pearson Australia Group Pty Ltd)
Penguin Books India Pvt Ltd, 11 Community Centre, Panchsheel Park, New Delhi – 110 017, India
Penguin Group (NZ), 67 Apollo Drive, Rosedale, Auckland 0632, New Zealand
(a division of Pearson New Zealand Ltd)
Penguin Books (South Africa) (Pty) Ltd, Block D, Rosebank Office Park, 181 Jan Smuts Avenue,
Parktown North, Gauteng 2193, South Africa

Penguin Books Ltd, Registered Offices: 80 Strand, London WC2R ORL, England

puffinbooks.com

First published in the English language in the USA by Amulet Books, an imprint of ABRAMS, 2013
Original English title: *Diary of a Wimpy Kid: Hard Luck*
(All rights reserved in all countries by Harry N. Abrams, Inc.)
Published simultaneously in Great Britain by Puffin Books 2013

001

Book design by Jeff Kinney
Cover design by Chad W. Beckerman and Jeff Kinney

The moral right of the author/illustrator has been asserted

Made and printed in China

British Library Cataloguing in Publication Data
A CIP catalogue record for this book is available from the British Library

ISBN: 978-0-141-35238-1

TO CHARLIE

Monday

Mom's always saying that friends will come and go but family is forever. Well, if that's true, I could be in for a rough ride.

I mean, I love my family and all, but I'm just not sure we were meant to LIVE together. Maybe it'll be better later on when we're all in different houses and only see each other on holidays, but right now things are just a little dicey.

I'm surprised Mom's always pushing the "family" message, since she and her sisters don't really get along. Maybe she thinks if she keeps repeating it to me and my brothers, then we'll come out different. But, if I was her, I wouldn't hold my breath.

I think Mom is just trying to make me feel better about my situation with Rowley anyway. Rowley's been my best friend ever since he moved into my neighbourhood, but things have really changed between us recently.

And it's all because of a GIRL.

Believe me, the last person in the world I ever thought would get a girlfriend was ROWLEY.

I always thought I'D be the one in a relationship and Rowley would be the guy everyone kind of felt sorry for.

I guess I've got to give Rowley some credit for actually finding a girl who likes him. But I don't have to be HAPPY about it.

Back in the good old days, it was just me and Rowley, and we hung out and did whatever we wanted. If we felt like blowing bubbles in our chocolate milk at lunch, then that's exactly what we did.

But now that there's a girl in the picture things are TOTALLY different.

Wherever Rowley is, his girlfriend Abigail is, too. And even if she ISN'T there it SEEMS like she is. I invited Rowley to my house for a sleepover last weekend so the two of us could spend some time together, but after about two hours I gave up trying to have any fun.

And when the two of them are in the same place it's even WORSE. Ever since Rowley and Abigail got together, it's like Rowley doesn't even have his own OPINIONS any more.

I was hoping this would've all blown over by now and things would be back to normal, but there's no sign of this ending anytime soon.

If you ask me, it's ALREADY gone too far. I've started noticing little changes in Rowley, like the way he combs his hair and the clothes he wears. And, I GUARANTEE you, Abigail is behind all of it.

But I'M the one who's been best friends with Rowley all these years, so if anyone has the right to change him it's ME.

I just don't get how you can go from being someone's best friend to getting kicked to the kerb. But that's exactly what happened.

During the winter, me and Rowley stored up some snowballs in my freezer so we could have a snowball fight when the weather got warm.

Well, yesterday was the first nice day we've had in forever, but when I went over to Rowley's house he acted like he was too good for me.

The thing is, I can honestly say I've been nice to Abigail, but SHE doesn't like ME. She's been trying to drive a wedge between me and Rowley ever since the two of them became a couple.

But whenever I try to bring the topic up with Rowley I get the same thing every time.

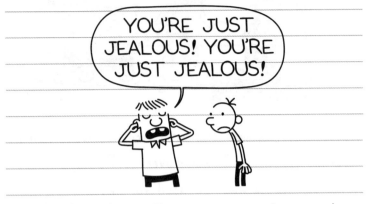

I wish I could give Rowley a piece of my mind, but I CAN'T because I'm depending on him to get me through the school year.

I have Mr Blakely for English, and he makes us turn in all our assignments in cursive. But it really hurts my hand when I write in cursive for too long, so I've been paying Rowley one peanut-butter cracker for every page that he transcribes for me.

But if I have to start writing my OWN assignments the handwriting on my homework won't be the same as before, and Mr Blakely will know.

So I'm stuck with Rowley, at least until I can find someone who can write exactly like him and who also likes peanut-butter crackers.

But the biggest problem with this Abigail situation isn't the English homework, it's the walk to school. Me and Rowley used to head in together every morning, but now Rowley goes over to Abigail's neighbourhood and walks to school with HER.

This is an issue for a COUPLE of reasons. For one, me and Rowley have a deal where he's in charge of scouting ahead for dog poop on the pavement. And that arrangement has saved me a BUNCH of times.

There's this one dog that really has it in for me and Rowley, and we have to keep our guard up whenever we pass by his house. He's this really mean Rottweiler named Rebel, and he used to get out of his yard and chase us on our way to school.

Rebel's owner had to install an electric fence to make sure he couldn't get loose. Now Rebel can't chase us, because if he takes one step out of his yard he'll get a shock from his collar.

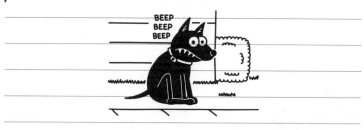

Ever since me and Rowley found out about Rebel's electric collar, we've been having some fun with him.

But Rebel figured out that as long as his COLLAR doesn't cross over the property line he won't get shocked.

11

And if I didn't have Rowley watching out for me I definitely would've stepped on one of Rebel's land mines by now.

The other reason it stinks that Rowley isn't walking with me is because, with the school year winding down, the teachers have really been loading us up with homework lately.

That means I have to take almost all my books home with me every day.

My body's not built to carry that kind of weight, but Rowley is practically like a pack animal, so it's no problem for HIM.

12

Unfortunately, Rowley is just as willing to help Abigail with HER books, which makes me think the only reason she's even with him is to USE him.

And, as Rowley's good friend, I find that a little hard to take.

<u>Tuesday</u>

I figured out a pretty good solution to my book problem. This morning I borrowed the wheelie case Dad uses when he goes on trips, and carrying all my school stuff was no sweat.

I was able to make pretty good time, too, but that's partially because I walked a little extra fast when I went by Mr Sandoval's house.

Before a snowstorm, Mr Sandoval always puts poles in the ground on either side of his driveway so the guy who ploughs it knows where the tarmac is.

The last time it snowed, me and Rowley plucked the poles out of Mr Sandoval's yard and started horsing around with them.

But I guess we didn't put the sticks back in exactly the right place, because when the guy came to plough Mr Sandoval's driveway he was off by about ten feet.

Mr Sandoval has been waiting for me and Rowley to show our faces in front of his house again so he can let us have it, but I'm not ready for that conversation just yet. ESPECIALLY not by myself.

Mr Sandoval's not the ONLY danger between my house and school, though.

Ever since they started doing construction on Gramma's street, we've had to take a detour on the walk home. And that brings us right by the woods where the Mingo kids hang out.

I don't actually know a whole lot about the Mingo kids. I've never seen any of them in school, so for all I know they just live in the woods like a pack of wild animals.

I'm not even sure if there are any parents or grown-ups in the whole Mingo clan. I've heard their leader is this boy named Meckley who always wears a vest and a belt with a gigantic metal buckle on it.

MECKLEY MINGO

One time me and Rowley got too close to the woods and one of the Mingo kids came out to let us know.

I'm still not sure what he meant by that, but if Meckley's belt buckle was gonna be involved in any way I didn't want to stick around to find out.

Now that I'm walking home on my own, I have to cross to the other side of the street when I get near the Mingos' woods. It wouldn't be a big deal except there's no pavement over there, and that can't be good for Dad's wheelie case.

Mom's noticed I haven't been hanging out with Rowley lately. She said I shouldn't get too worked up over it because most friendships from childhood don't last and that me and Rowley will probably grow apart over the years anyway.

Well, I hope that's not true, because I think it's important for me to keep my childhood friends so that later on someone can appreciate how far I've come.

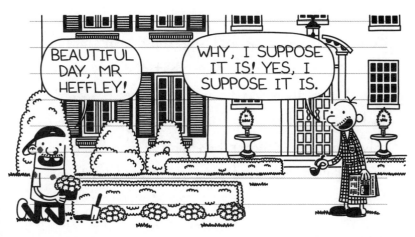

19

I'm not so sure Mom's qualified to give me friendship advice anyway, because guy friendships are TOTALLY different from girl friendships. And I know because I've read almost every single book in the Slumber Party Pals series.

Before you judge me and say those books are for GIRLS, let me just explain that the only reason I got into them was because one time I forgot to bring in a book for Silent Reading, and the only books the teacher had were in the Slumber Party Pals series. And once you've read ONE of them you can't stop.

There must be something like a hundred books in that series. The first thirty or so were pretty good, but after that I think the author started running out of ideas.

Anyway, in the Slumber Party Pals books these two friends are always getting into fights with each other about little stuff.

But after a while things always cool down and the girls learn the true meaning of friendship.

And that's basically the plot of every single book in the Slumber Party Pals series. Well, that might be the way things work with GIRLS, but I can tell you firsthand that it's NOT the way it works with BOYS.

For boys, things are just a lot less complicated. For example, let's say one guy breaks something that belongs to another guy, but it's totally an accident. Well, five seconds later everybody's moved on and things are pretty much back to normal.

I don't know if that means guys are less sophisticated than girls or whatever, but I DO know that the way we do things sure saves a lot of time and energy.

Friday
I hate to say it, but Mom's prediction about me and Rowley is starting to come true.

Ever since Abigail and Rowley got together, Abigail has been sitting at our lunch table, which is all boys. I already mentioned how she's not a fan of the chocolate-milk bubble-blowing thing, but there's a lot of OTHER stuff she doesn't like either.

One of them is the Five-Second Rule. All the guys at our table agree that if you drop a piece of food on the floor, as long as you pick it up within five seconds, it's still OK to eat.

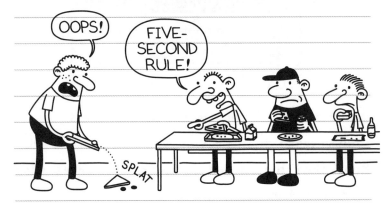

A new twist someone came up with recently is that you can grab a piece of food off the floor even if YOU'RE not the one who actually DROPPED it. I've lost two chocolate-chip cookies and a Fudgsicle that way already.

This new rule has caused some other problems, though. Yesterday, Freddie Harlahan ate a piece of ham off the floor because he thought Carl Dumas dropped it, but it was actually there from the group that had lunch BEFORE us.

It might've even been there from before THAT, because Freddie started to feel sick and ended up in the nurse's office for the rest of the day.

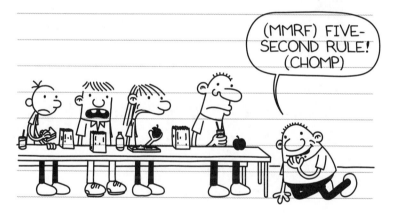

(MMRF) FIVE-SECOND RULE! (CHOMP)

Something tells me they don't have the Five-Second Rule at the table Abigail used to sit at, or probably any of the OTHER girls' tables. Another thing I'll bet they don't have is French Fry Fridays.

They serve burgers in the cafeteria every Friday, but the meat is grey and tastes like a wet sponge. PLUS, they serve sweet-potato fries now instead of regular french fries.

But Nolan Tiago's mom works part-time in the library, and every Friday she brings Nolan a cheeseburger and fries from the fast-food place on the corner.

Nolan eats his fries, but he always lets the rest of us have whatever falls out into the bag. And I've seen kids practically come to blows over a few cold french fries.

We decided the only way to prevent someone from getting hurt was to split the fries up evenly, so we brought in Alex Aruda to divvy them up and give everyone an equal number.

The rest of us keep an eye on Alex to make sure he's not taking any extra for himself.

Some kids eat all their fries at once, but I nibble mine real slow to make them last as long as possible.

But no matter how many fries we get it's never enough. Today there were only THREE fries in the bag, and we had to split them ten ways.

So you had a couple of kids paying Nolan a dime each just to smell the fries on his breath. And I think that's what made Abigail finally decide to look for another place to sit.

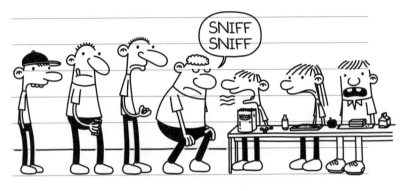

When Abigail moved to a different table, she took Rowley with her. But that's fine with ME because it means more french fries for the rest of us.

Abigail and Rowley moved to the Couples Table, which is the only place in the whole cafeteria where there's still room to sit. After the Valentine's Day dance, almost all the couples in our grade broke up, so Rowley and Abigail didn't have any trouble finding a spot.

The reason the couples have a whole table all to themselves is because no one else can stand to be around them. Let me just say that you couldn't PAY me to sit and watch Abigail feed Rowley his pudding every day.

SLURP SMACK

The SECOND that Rowley and Abigail left our table, two guys slid right into their empty spots. There aren't enough seats in the cafeteria for all the kids in our lunch period, so there's actually a line to get one.

If you didn't get a seat on the first day of school, you were out of luck. There are some kids who have been waiting since September, and they'll probably STILL be waiting for a seat on the last day of school.

I feel pretty lucky I got a seat, because the people who didn't get one have to find a place to sit anywhere they can.

The kids in the middle of the line have pretty much given up hope that they're gonna get a seat, so some of them have started selling their spots to the kids behind them. I heard that Brady Connor sold his position at the number-fifteen spot to Glenn Harris, who was one spot back, for five dollars and an ice-cream sandwich.

Unfortunately for me, the two kids in the front of the line were Earl Dremmell and his twin brother, Andy, and they took Abigail and Rowley's spots. Earl and Andy have Phys Ed right before lunch, and those guys both fake their gym showers, just like I do.

Even though I sit at a table with a bunch of guys, I wouldn't call any of them my actual FRIENDS. Because when we head outside for recess, we all go our separate ways.

I USED to hang out with Rowley during recess, but those days are over. It's probably time for me to strike out on my own, but the problem is I don't know where I'm supposed to go.

First of all, there are some kids I have to watch out for on the playground.

A few years ago Mom invited a bunch of my classmates to my birthday party, but she thought I already had enough toys and she said so on the invitation.

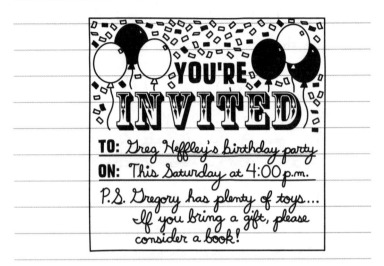

**YOU'RE INVITED**

**TO:** Greg Heffley's birthday party
**ON:** This Saturday at 4:00 p.m.

P.S. Gregory has plenty of toys...
If you bring a gift, please
consider a book!

Usually, when you open presents at your birthday party, all the other kids are jealous. But at MY party I think people just felt sorry for me.

Unfortunately, Mom's idea caught on with a bunch of OTHER moms in our neighbourhood, and nowadays I have to be careful whenever I see a kid walking around at recess carrying a new book.

Then there's Leon Feast and HIS gang. I got into a situation with those guys a few summers ago, and there's been bad blood between us ever since.

One day me and Rowley went down to the school to ride our bikes on the basketball court, but Leon and his friends showed up a few minutes later.

They told us that we were gonna have to leave so they could play basketball.

I told Leon we could make a compromise and they could have one half of the court and we could ride our bikes on the other. But they didn't like THAT idea and gave us the boot.

On the ride home I was really mad that we let ourselves get pushed around like that, and I wanted to DO something about it. A few days later Mom asked me out of the blue if I wanted her to sign me up for the "Superhero Training Academy". She showed me the flyer, and I was sold.

I couldn't WAIT to graduate from the Superhero Training Academy and show Leon and his gang a thing or two.

Rowley's mom signed HIM up, too, and we were both pretty excited about it. But on the first day I realized it was a total scam.

First of all, the Superhero Training Academy was in the gymnastics room at the YMCA and not some secret bunker underneath the building. Then I found out the whole "superpower" part was a joke.

So me and Rowley were stuck in day camp for a week while our moms ran errands. And at the end we didn't even get masks or costumes or anything cool like that. We just got these stupid certificates.

**Gregory Heffley**

IS A

# Superhero

OF

showing good manners during snack time.

**Zap!**

A few weeks later we went down to the school on our bikes again and, sure enough, Leon and his friends were on the basketball court. But I guess I should've given Rowley the heads-up that his "superhero training" was totally worthless.

Aside from the kids I need to avoid, like Leon, there are a few different groups that hang out together at recess. But I don't think I really fit in with any of them.

There are some kids who play a fantasy-card game and another group that just hangs out and reads.

Then there's the group that plays on the field. A few months ago the school banned any games that involve a ball because too many kids were getting hurt.

So these guys made up a game where somebody's SHOE is the ball. But don't even ask me what the point of the game is.

Erick Glick hangs out with his sketchy friends behind the school where the teachers can't see them. I've heard that if you want to buy an old book report or homework assignment, he's the guy to talk to.

The GIRLS hang out in groups, too. There's one that jumps rope near the side of the school and another that does hopscotch fifty feet away. I've heard the two groups don't get along, but I have no idea what that's all about.

I'll tell you the group I WISH I could join, and that's the girls who hang out near the cafeteria door and gossip about everyone who walks by.

I've tried to slip into that group before, but it's pretty clear outsiders aren't welcome.

The only place where boys and girls hang out TOGETHER is on the playground. Some of the kids have started playing Girls Chase Boys, which was a big thing back in elementary school.

I've tried to get in on the Girls Chase Boys game over the years, but most of the girls are only interested in chasing the POPULAR guys like Bryce Anderson.

Every so often during Girls Chase Boys, somebody will yell out and flip the whole game.

It goes back and forth like that until the bell rings and it's time to go inside.

The only problem with that game is they never say what you're supposed to do when you actually CATCH someone. I remember the time in fifth grade when we were playing Boys Chase Girls and I caught Cara Punter fair and square.

Cara reported me to the playground monitor, who made me sit against the wall for the rest of recess. I'm pretty sure the school called my PARENTS, too.

I think the school realized there are some kids who have trouble joining in with the others at recess, so a few weeks ago they turned the bully-reporting station on the playground into a "Find a Friend" station.

I always thought the Find a Friend station was a lame idea, but it's not like I have a lot of options these days.

I don't know if people didn't notice the blue light going off or if everyone was just too busy playing Girls Chase Boys, but no kids came over. I think Mr Nern must've felt sorry for me, because he walked over with a box of checkers.

I guess it was better than nothing. But I hope Mr Nern doesn't think this is gonna be a regular thing.

<u>Wednesday</u>

OK, you KNOW things are bad when even your little brother has more friends than you.

A family with a kindergarten-age kid named Mikey moved in down the street a few weeks ago, and Mikey and Manny hit it off. The two of them have been hanging out after school every day since they met.

Mikey loves to drink grape juice, and I've never seen him without a juice ring round his lips. So he always looks like a forty-year-old man with a goatee.

MIKEY

The only thing Mikey and Manny do together is watch TV.

As far as I know, neither of them has ever said a single word to the other, but I guess something about their relationship just works.

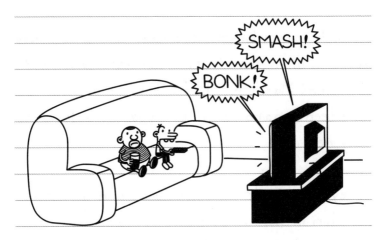

And, even crazier than that, now GRANDPA has a girlfriend. I didn't even know you could still DATE once you got to be Grandpa's age, but I guess I was wrong.

I probably shouldn't be surprised. Dad says that at Leisure Towers the women outnumber the men ten to one. So there are always women lined up at Grandpa's door trying to win him over with casseroles and baked goods.

Grandpa started dating this widow named Darlene, and we met her this weekend when they came over for dinner.

I think it's totally crazy that Rowley and Grandpa both have girlfriends at the same time.

All I can say is that if these are the people who are gonna populate the next generation the human race is in BIG trouble.

I never should've opened up to Mom about what's been going on in my social life, because now she's made it her mission to help me find new friends.

Yesterday she invited her old roommate from college to our house because her friend has a son and Mom thought the two of us might really "hit it off".

But what Mom DIDN'T mention is that her friend's son is a high school SENIOR, which made for a really awkward afternoon.

Lately Mom's been giving me tips on how to make new friends at school.

I think her heart is in the right place, but the advice she gives me would NEVER work with kids my age. For example, Mom said that if I'm just really nice to everyone I meet, then word will spread and I'll become the most popular kid at school in no time.

Maybe that kind of stuff worked when Mom was growing up, but kids aren't like that any more. I keep telling Mom that NOWADAYS popularity is based on stuff like what kinds of clothes you wear and what kind of mobile phone you have. But she doesn't want to hear it.

At school there's this big push to encourage "positive reinforcement", so they've started taking down all the anti-bullying posters in the hallways because they don't fit with the new theme.

Now, instead of punishing kids for acting mean to each other, they're rewarding kids for being NICE.

The basic idea is that if a teacher catches you being kind to another kid you get a "Hero Point".

If you get a certain number of Hero Points you can turn them in for prizes like extra recess time.

And the homeroom that gets the MOST Hero Points gets a day off from school in June.

I actually thought it was a pretty decent idea, but of course people always have to go and mess things up. Right away kids realized they didn't actually have to do good deeds to get Hero Points. They just started FAKING good deeds whenever the teachers were around.

Hero Points are printed on sheets of ten, and teachers tear one off when they want to reward a kid.

Erick Glick got his hands on one of the sheets and photocopied it, so after that there were all these counterfeit Hero Points going around school.

Erick started selling them for twenty-five cents a point, but then other kids realized THEY could make copies, too, and after that there were so many Hero Points going around that you could buy a HUNDRED for a QUARTER.

The teachers got suspicious when the worst kids in our class started turning in tons of Hero Points for extra recess.

So the school invalidated all the Hero Points printed on white paper and created a whole new batch on GREEN paper. But it didn't take long for people to start making copies on green paper, and the whole thing started all over again.

Every time the school changed the colour of the paper, there would be fakes made within twenty-four hours. Finally, the school started punishing kids who turned in more than five Hero Points at a time, because the teachers saw that as proof they were counterfeit.

But THAT wasn't fair, either. Marcel Templeton, one of the nicest kids in our class, got put in detention for the rest of the month even though he'd earned his thirty-five Hero Points legitimately.

Eventually, the janitor busted one of the main counterfeit operations when he walked into an empty Science room that kids were using as their base.

The school cancelled the whole Hero Points programme after that, which stinks because now that extra recess is off the table nobody's willing to do anything nice.

<u>Sunday</u>
I think Mom took that stuff I said about popularity with kids my age to heart, because today she took me out clothes shopping.

Ordinarily I can't STAND going clothes shopping, because the only time we do it is at the beginning of the school year. And once a year is enough for ME.

I've done a lot of boring things in my life, but NOTHING saps my energy more than back-to-school clothes shopping.

Usually, Mom takes us shopping at this place downtown called Frugal Freddy's. I think the people who run that store understand guys, because they give us our own little area to sit in while the women shop.

Last September Mom took me and Rodrick to Frugal Freddy's and picked out all our clothes for us. Unfortunately, she forgot to come GET us after she was done shopping, and she got all the way home before she realized it.

We must've been in there for three hours before Mom came back to get us.

Well, today I was actually EXCITED to go clothes shopping. I got two pairs of jeans and three shirts, but the thing I was most pumped about was the SHOES.

All of my shoes are hand-me-downs from Rodrick, and whenever I get a pair of HIS shoes I have to spend a few hours scraping the bubble gum off the bottoms.

The only time I had a new pair of shoes was in fourth grade when Mom got me some trainers for the first day of school.

I told her I'd never heard of "Sportzterz" before. She told me they were from Europe and had "space-age technology". So I was all proud of my new shoes when I went to school.

But at recess the rubber soles on both shoes fell clean off. I was upset, and when I got home I showed Mom, who said not to worry and that we'd take them back to the store and get new ones.

That's when I found out she'd bought the shoes at the dollar store and the whole "space-age technology" thing was just a bunch of baloney.

When Mom said she was taking me shoe shopping today, I made sure she knew I was only interested in name brands.

It wasn't easy deciding which shoes to get, though. There are about a million different types, and each one is supposedly good for a specific thing.

There are shoes for hiking, shoes for running, shoes for skateboarding, and a bunch of other ones, too.

There was a pair of fancy high-tech basketball shoes I really liked. They had some sort of thing in the soles that's supposed to make you jump higher, and I was seriously thinking about getting them.

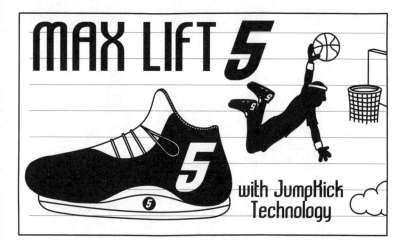

MAX LIFT **5**

with JumpKick Technology

But I got nervous that if I bought those I'd be totally out of control on the walk to school.

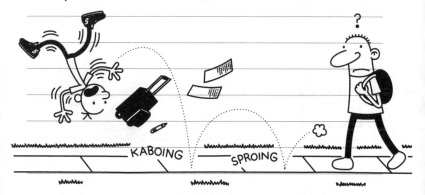

KABOING  SPROING

Then there was a pair of green "cross-training" shoes that really looked awesome, but on the box it said they were for the "serious athlete".

So if I got those I think they'd just be wasted on me.

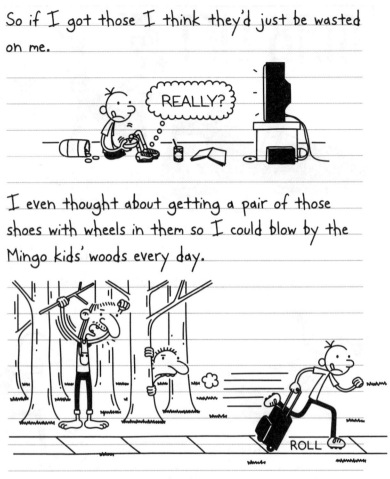

I even thought about getting a pair of those shoes with wheels in them so I could blow by the Mingo kids' woods every day.

ROLL

I finally decided on some shoes that were sporty but not too over-the-top. Mom asked me if I wanted to wear them home, but there was no WAY I was gonna let my shoes get dirty before I wore them to school for the first time.

64

Plus, it gave me a chance to enjoy the new-shoe smell all the way home.

Monday

I never noticed how DIRTY the ground is until I got my new shoes. And not just the actual ground but the street and the SIDEWALK, too.

The way to school is like a minefield of mud and grease and other junk, and you practically have to be a ninja to avoid all of it.

In fact, after getting only one block from
my house this morning, I turned round and
went back inside. I got some of those plastic
grocery bags to put my feet in, and for a while
everything was good.

But eventually the bottoms of the bags got
shredded, and then they didn't give me any
protection at ALL. So I just ripped the rest
of the bags off and threw them in the nearest
trash can.

After that I did my best to avoid the danger areas. I stayed on the pavement until I realized I was getting pebbles in the little grooves of my shoes, and I knew those were gonna take FOREVER to dig out with a stick. So I tried to minimize the amount of rubber that touched the cement.

Eventually, I gave up and just walked on the grass. By the time I got to school, I was twenty minutes late, but it was totally worth it to show up in style.

Unfortunately, we were having a pop quiz in Geography, and I had to try and catch up to everyone else.

A few minutes into the quiz, I noticed a really terrible smell. At first I thought it was Bernard Barnson, who usually doesn't smell too good in general.

But this was WAY worse than usual. I took my stuff to a desk at the back of the room so I could concentrate on my quiz, but the smell FOLLOWED me. And that's when I realized where it was REALLY coming from.

I must've stepped in dog poop when I walked on the grass. And I knew EXACTLY where it had happened, too.

I took my shoe off and went to the front of the room to tell Mrs Pope about my situation.

But I think Mrs Pope thought I was trying to skip out on the pop quiz, because she gave me a plastic bag to put my shoe in and told me to return to my seat.

By now the rest of the kids had figured out what was going on, and everyone had a good laugh at my expense.

Usually, I find poop as funny as the next guy, but that's when someone ELSE steps in it.

In fact, the best time I ever had with Rowley was on the Fourth of July when his parents took us downtown to see the fireworks. We had to get there a few hours early to set up our blanket in the park.

One of the police horses unloaded right on the main path where everybody was walking by, and the two of us spent the rest of the night watching people's reactions as they tried to avoid it.

Those were some good times, but I guess they're all over now.

What really makes me mad is that if everything was the way it was SUPPOSED to be I would've been walking to school with Rowley this morning and he would've been doing his job of scouting ahead.

But Rowley had to go and get himself a girlfriend, and now I guess I'M the one who has to suffer.

I had tracked Rebel's mess all over the classroom, and they had to call in Mr Meeks to clean it up. He kept shooting me dirty looks, which made it really tough to concentrate on my pop quiz.

After class ended I went to the front office to see if there was anything they could do to help me. The school secretary let me look through the Lost and Found box for a replacement shoe, but the only thing in there that even came close was a girl's winter boot.

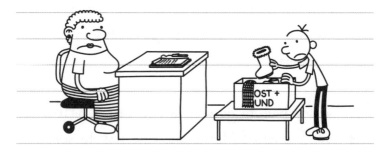

Right then Mr Nern came out of the teachers'
lounge, and the secretary asked him if he happened
to have any spare shoes. Mr Nern said he
actually had an extra pair in his office, and he
went to get one for me.

I never noticed before, but Mr Nern has some
GIGANTIC feet. And I hope just because he
lent me his shoes doesn't mean I have to keep
playing checkers with him at recess.

FLOP
FLOP

<u>Wednesday</u>

Since I'm not hanging out with Rowley after
school any more, I've got a LOT more time on
my hands. But the thing I've learned is that you
should never tell your mom you've got nothing to do.

So I've been going outside after school just to
avoid doing chores at home. Mom's been telling
me I should "branch out" and try to find new
friends in the neighbourhood, but where I live the
pickings are pretty slim.

A few houses down are the Lasky boys, but
THEIR idea of a good time is stripping down to
their underwear and wrestling in the front yard.

Diagonally across the street is a kid named Mitchell Flammer, who I think is a year or two younger than me. But I don't even know what he LOOKS like, because I've never seen him without a motorcycle helmet on.

A few houses down on the right, you've got Aric Holbert, who was suspended three weeks ago for breaking in and vandalizing the school.

He tried to deny it was him, but it was pretty pointless.

Then there's Fregley, who lives a few houses up from me. If there's anything GOOD that's come out of my situation in the past few weeks, it's that I haven't had to walk by Fregley's house on my way up to see Rowley.

Unfortunately, Mom's always trying to set up a "playdate" between me and Fregley. She says she feels bad for him because he seems like a "lonely boy".

I really wish Mom wouldn't say things like that, because then it makes me feel all guilty. And, trust me, I already feel bad ENOUGH seeing Fregley out on the playground every day.

But today I had a really crazy thought: I realized that, if I became friends with Fregley, I could mould him into EXACTLY the type of friend I wanted.

I could basically take all the things I like about Rowley and teach Fregley how to do them. Plus, Fregley could bring something EXTRA to the table.

I've noticed that at my school the most popular guys have a funny sidekick. One of the boys in Bryce Anderson's entourage is Jeffrey Laffley, and I GUARANTEE you the only reason Bryce keeps Jeffrey around is for comic relief.

And girls NEVER go for the funny sidekick, so Fregley wouldn't even be a threat to me.

I'll just need to make sure people think Fregley is acting funny on PURPOSE. Because with him you can never really tell.

Today at lunch I went to find Fregley and invite him to sit at our table. He was so far back in the line to get a seat that he was out in the hallway near the boys' bathroom.

Luckily, Fregley is pretty skinny, so we were able to squeeze him in. The first thing I did was tell him how things worked, starting with the Five-Second Rule.

I was right in the middle of telling him how you can claim a piece of food that doesn't belong to you, when Fregley went for the crisp in my hand with no warning.

I was pretty mad, and I told Fregley that if he was gonna pull that kind of nonsense he could go back to his spot on the floor in the hallway.

I explained that somebody had to actually DROP something before it could be claimed. He seemed to get it and sort of tried to apologize, so I guess you'd have to call that progress.

While Fregley was eating lunch, I sneaked a peek at his notebook to see how good his cursive was. But when I saw what was on the first page I wished I hadn't.

After school, I asked Fregley if he wanted to walk home with me. I explained how I needed him to scout ahead for dog poop, and how he'll have to pull my wheelie case from time to time. Fregley seemed eager to help out, and things started off pretty smoothly.

But I wasn't paying attention, and I forgot to cross the street when we got near the Mingo kids' woods. So the next thing we knew we had the whole pack of them chasing after us.

We finally lost them when we got to the bottom of our street, but when Fregley gave my case back it was practically EMPTY.

I asked Fregley what happened to all my books, and he said he threw them out when the Mingo kids were chasing us. I asked him why he'd gone and done THAT, and he said he was hoping they'd stop and READ them.

So day one was a little bit of a disaster. But Fregley's gonna be a long-term project, and I'd better prepare myself for some bumps along the way.

Thursday

This morning me and Fregley were supposed to walk to school together, but at 8:30 he still hadn't shown up at my house. So I went over to his place and knocked on the front door.

Nobody answered, and I was about to just head to school by myself when I heard some noises inside like a bowling ball falling down the stairs. Then the front door opened, and Fregley was standing there.

Fregley told me that when he was getting dressed he accidentally put his shirt on upside down and got stuck. That meant it was up to ME to untangle him.

At first I was a little irritated, but then I realized this was just the kind of thing other people might find FUNNY.

So at lunch I brought Fregley over to one of the girls' tables and had him do the thing with his shirt again.

Unfortunately, we must've picked the wrong table, because not ONE of the girls even let out a chuckle.

I asked Fregley if he knew any jokes, but he said he didn't. Then I asked him if he knew how to do any tricks, and he pulled out a piece of bubble gum.

Fregley took off his shirt and put the gum in his belly button. I didn't know where this was going, so I took a few steps back. And then, no lie, he started CHEWING it.

I don't know if any of the girls were impressed, but I definitely was. Then Fregley said he was gonna blow a BUBBLE, which was something I HAD to see.

But I should've known it's not physically possible to blow a bubble with your belly button.

Word about Fregley's talent got around the cafeteria quick, and for the rest of the lunch period almost every boy in our class was at our table wanting to see what ELSE Fregley could chew.

In fact, it got so crowded there wasn't even a place for ME to sit.

So while Fregley was enjoying his moment in the spotlight I was eating my lunch out in the hallway.

This just goes to show that no matter how nice you are to some people they'll turn their back on you the second they get the chance.

CHEW
CHEW

Friday
With everything that's been going on at school, I've really been looking forward to spring break. I figure having a week to myself will be EXACTLY what the doctor ordered.

But tonight my plan for a stress-free week went out the window. When Dad asked Mom what we're doing for Easter this year, she said her family is coming to town.

I was TOTALLY blindsided by that news, and I could tell Dad felt the exact same way.

Mom NEVER tells us when her family is coming to visit, because she knows if she gives us too much advance warning we'll make a run for it.

Most of the relatives on Mom's side of the family live pretty far away, so we don't see them that often. I'm OK with that because whenever we DO see them I need plenty of time to recover.

I'm sure most families have their issues, but it seems like when it comes to Mom's side there's just a lot of extra drama.

Mom has four sisters, and they're so different from one another that it's kind of amazing they grew up under the same roof.

AUNT          AUNT          AUNT          AUNT
GRETCHEN      AUDRA        VERONICA       CAKEY

Mom's oldest sister is Aunt Cakey, who isn't married and doesn't have any children. And that's probably a good thing, because it's pretty obvious she doesn't like kids.

One time when I was little, Aunt Cakey came to stay with us, and Mom went out for a few hours and left me behind with her. But I don't think Aunt Cakey had ever been alone with a kid before, and she seemed on edge the whole time.

I guess she thought I was gonna break something, so the first thing she did was put everything that was fragile out of reach. Then she just stood there and watched me to make sure I didn't touch anything.

After about an hour, Aunt Cakey said it was time for me to take a nap. I tried to tell her I didn't really take naps any more, but she said it's rude to talk back to an adult.

Aunt Cakey said she'd be downstairs in the laundry room ironing and she'd come wake me up in a few hours.

Then she turned out the light, but just before
she shut the door she said –

WHATEVER YOU
DO, DON'T GO
DOWNSTAIRS
AND TOUCH
THE IRON.

The idea of touching the iron never would've
entered my mind, but once Aunt Cakey put it in my
head I couldn't stop thinking about it. So half
an hour later I sneaked downstairs like I was on
some kind of stealth mission.

Aunt Cakey was in the family room watching television, and I had to go past her to get into the laundry room.

Once I was in, I pulled out the little stool Mom uses to reach high places and pressed my whole hand on the iron.

Don't ask me WHAT I was thinking. I ended up with a second-degree burn, and Mom's never trusted Aunt Cakey to babysit again, which I'm sure is just fine with HER.

Mom's youngest sister is Aunt Gretchen, and she's the complete OPPOSITE of Aunt Cakey. Aunt Gretchen has twin boys named Malvin and Malcolm, who are TOTALLY wild. In fact, they're so out of control Aunt Gretchen used to keep them on child leashes.

One time when Aunt Gretchen and her kids visited, they brought their PETS with them. So it was like a zoo in our house.

Aunt Gretchen took off for a few days to go sightseeing, and we had to take care of her kids AND her animals. It got totally out of hand when her rabbit gave birth to a litter of bunnies two days before she got back.

BOING

Dad wasn't too happy about the situation, because Aunt Gretchen had told us her rabbit was a BOY.

I can deal with Aunt Gretchen's pets, but her sons are a whole OTHER matter.

On that same visit, Malvin and Malcolm played a game of catch in our driveway with a rock or a piece of concrete or something.

I admit I've done some dumb things in my life, but I don't think I've ever done anything as stupid as THAT.

YAAH!

Before you knew it, Mom had taken Malvin to the emergency room to get stitches in his forehead, and we were responsible for Malcolm.

While Mom was gone, Malcolm somehow managed to get hold of Dad's shaving kit, and by the time we found him there was nothing anybody could do about it.

Dad said if Aunt Gretchen and her boys are staying with us this time around he's gonna get a hotel room for himself. But Mom said we're family and family should be TOGETHER.

I'll tell you one person who WON'T be coming to Easter, though, and that's Aunt Veronica. She hasn't been to a family event in something like five years, or at least not in PERSON. I think being with the family stresses her out, so whenever there's a big gathering she makes her appearance by video conference.

In fact, I don't think I've seen her in the flesh
since I was three or four.

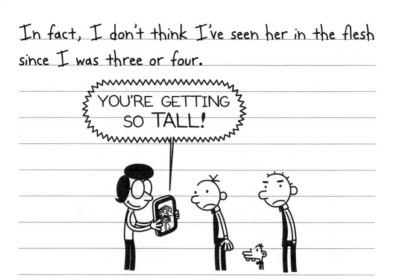

One summer we all got together for an outdoor
wedding. The ceremony lasted something like two
hours and it was really hot, and I could tell
Aunt Veronica was playing video games on her
computer the whole time.

The only aunt I haven't talked about yet is Aunt Audra. She's one of those people who believe in crystal balls and horoscopes and all that, and she doesn't do ANYTHING without talking to her psychic.

I know this firsthand because I stayed with her for two weeks a few summers back.

When Mom found out Aunt Audra took me along to her psychic appointments, she wasn't happy. Mom said all that fortune-telling stuff was just a bunch of "hocus-pocus" and that Aunt Audra was wasting her money.

But I had a FEELING Mom would say something like that.

I don't know what kind of training you need to become a psychic, but if there's not too much work involved, then I could totally see that as a career path for me.

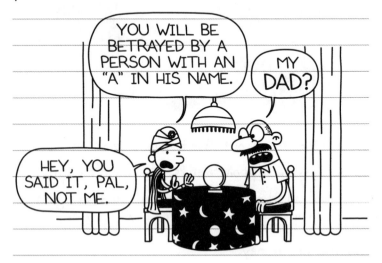

I'm kind of surprised Mom feels that way about fortune-telling and all that, because SHE'S the one who's always saying Gramma has ESP. I don't know if that's true or not, but if it IS, then Gramma's not using her powers to their full potential.

SO, GRAMMA, WHAT DO YOU THINK THE LOTTERY NUMBERS WILL BE TONIGHT?

I'M NOT SURE, BUT I "PREDICT" YOU'RE GOING TO ENJOY THESE COOKIES!

To be honest with you, I don't know how much I believe in that type of stuff myself. All I can say is that none of it has helped ME any.

When I was eight, we went on a family camping trip and stopped at a store that sold all sorts of souvenirs and trinkets.

Dad gave me three dollars to spend, and I used it all to buy a rabbit's foot, which was supposed to bring me good luck.

But on that trip I got food poisoning AND sprained my ankle. So I got rid of the rabbit's foot the first chance I got.

It's just as well, because I was uncomfortable carrying that thing around anyway. I realized that if I ended up winning the lottery or something because of my rabbit's foot I wouldn't really be able to enjoy it.

WELL, CONGRATULATIONS!

Whenever Dad leaves the newspaper out on the kitchen table, I always read my horoscope. But there's never any information in it I can actually USE.

> When Saturn aligns with Jupiter, beware a stranger who carries ill tidings. Meanwhile, a person you once carried a flame for now admires you from afar. Your lucky numbers are 1,2,4,5,7 & 126.

And fortune cookies are even MORE worthless. We used to go to the Chinese restaurant in the centre of town on Christmas Eve, and I was always excited to open my cookie to see what the future held for me.

But here's the fortune I got the last time I was there -

You will buy some new pants.

I mean, whoever wrote THAT one wasn't even TRYING.

See, what I NEED is something that actually TELLS me what to do, so I don't have to guess. Up to this point, I've been making all my own decisions, and I'm not super happy with the results.

## Wednesday

I actually used to look FORWARD to when Mom's family came to town, because it was a good way for me to make some cash.

One year I was drawing pictures at the kitchen table, and Mom told me I should try selling my drawings to the family.

It actually worked out GREAT. I'd draw a picture of a house or a turtle, and turn round and sell it to someone in the family for five bucks.

WOW, YOU ARE AN **AMAZING** ARTIST, GREGORY!

In the weeks leading up to a big family holiday, I'd draw as fast as I could so I had a big stockpile when my relatives arrived. One Thanksgiving I drew so many pictures that I made eighty dollars.

In fact, it was so easy to turn my art into cash that I thought that's how it was gonna be for the rest of my life.

But once I got a little older the same relatives who were snapping up my drawings when I was little weren't as quick to pull out their wallets.

And I'm still not sure if it's because I went back to the same people too many times or because I'd doubled my prices.

But when Manny started selling HIS drawings all of a sudden my relatives were like human ATM machines.

Let me just say this: when I draw a picture, I put a lot of time and effort into it. But Manny scribbles out fifteen drawings in a minute, and don't even ask me what half of them are supposed to BE.

This all just goes to show that some people have no taste when it comes to art.

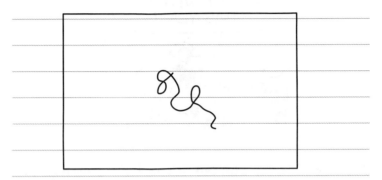

Thursday

We're having Easter at Gramma's house again this year, which kind of stinks, because Gramma's house isn't very kid-friendly. The only thing she has that's even CLOSE to a toy over there is this stuffed elephant called Ellie.

Gramma bought Ellie as a chew toy for our old dog, Sweetie, who lives with her now.

But Sweetie tore off Ellie's trunk, ears and legs on the first day he had it. So now you can't even tell it's supposed to be an elephant.

If you're a kid, that's all you've got for entertainment at Gramma's house. And there's only so much fun you can have with a stuffed bowling pin.

POKE

It wouldn't be so boring at Gramma's if Sweetie could still PLAY like he used to. But Gramma has fed him so much dog food and table scraps that at this point he's basically a beach ball with legs.

PLUS, Gramma dresses him up like a little person now, so I think he's just really depressed.

Every once in a while when we have dinner over at Gramma's, we try and have a little fun with Sweetie anyway.

One night we found out that if you sneak up behind him when he's sleeping and make a raspberry sound with your lips, his ears perk up.

Then Sweetie sniffs his rear end for the next five minutes and goes back to sleep.

Me and Rodrick do that over and over, and Sweetie has the EXACT same reaction every single time. But one night when Dad gave it a try it TOTALLY backfired.

Even though Gramma's house is boring, Easter actually used to be pretty fun. When Great Granny Meemaw was still alive, we'd always have a big Easter egg hunt at Gramma's.

MEEMAW

Meemaw was Gramma's mom. No disrespect to Meemaw or anything, but if I ever have grandkids I'M gonna be the one who chooses what they call me, not THEM.

And I'm gonna go with something basic like "Grandpa" or "Grandad", because I don't want to end up getting stuck with some goofy nickname for the rest of my life.

I'm sure my great grandfather wishes he could change his name, but he's about ninety-three years old, so there's really no point now.

Anyway, Meemaw was in charge of putting prizes in the plastic eggs for the Easter egg hunt. She'd stuff them with things like candy and change, but every so often she'd drop in a five-dollar bill.

Then she'd hide the eggs inside Gramma's house and in her backyard.

After Easter brunch, all of us kids would go to Gramma's backyard and get ready to fill up our baskets with as many eggs as we could find.

Meemaw used to overdo it with the eggs, though, and hide WAY more than she needed to. In fact, I'll bet you could go out in Gramma's backyard right now and STILL find enough to fill up a basket.

Sometimes I'll find an egg at Gramma's in a cabinet or stuffed between the couch cushions. A few weeks ago Gramma's toilet wasn't working, and Dad found a pink plastic egg in the water tank that had probably been bobbing around in there for YEARS.

When Meemaw got older she wasn't as sharp as she used to be, and she started putting strange things in the plastic eggs for prizes.

One year I found a green bean, a bottle cap and a paper clip in my eggs. That was the same year Manny found dental floss in one of HIS.

And I can tell you from experience that a used tissue sounds EXACTLY the same as a five-dollar bill when it's inside a plastic egg.

SHAKE
SHAKE

The last Easter egg hunt we had was the year Meemaw passed away. At her funeral, Mom realized Meemaw wasn't wearing her diamond wedding ring.

Everybody was all in a panic because that ring had been in the family for three generations, and apparently it was worth a lot of money.

After the funeral the family went to the rest home where Meemaw and Peepaw lived and turned the place upside down, but they couldn't find the ring anywhere.

It got pretty ugly after that. Great Aunt Beatrice accused her sister, Great Aunt Martha, of pocketing the ring for herself. Then Aunt Gretchen said Meemaw promised HER the ring, so if anybody found it, they needed to hand it over.

And, before you knew it, the whole family was at each other's throats.

So that's how things ended the last time we all got together, and it's probably the reason we haven't been in one place since.

I think the whole ring situation really shook Mom up. She said she hopes NO ONE finds Meemaw's ring, because if someone DOES it could break up the whole family.

But if that means no more visits from Aunt Gretchen and her kids I have to say I'm all for it.

Sunday
When it comes to holidays, I'm more of a Christmas guy than an Easter guy.

On Christmas, the second you get home from church, you can just totally unwind.

But on Easter you have to stay in your church clothes the whole day, or at least you do in MY family. Today we went straight from church to Gramma's house, and my tie was ALREADY starting to drive me crazy.

119

I was nervous everyone was just gonna pick right back up where they left off after Meemaw's funeral, but when we got to Gramma's everyone seemed to have moved past it.

I've never been that comfortable walking into a room full of relatives. I know I see these people once or twice a year, but there are so many of them I can't even remember everyone's NAME. They all seem to remember everything about ME, though.

SO HOW DID YOU END UP DOING ON THAT STATE CAPITALS TEST?

I always try to get past the crowd in the front hallway as quickly as possible and find a place where there aren't as many people.

Manny's strategy is to pretend he doesn't speak whenever he's at family gatherings. I admit I'm a little jealous and wish I had come up with that idea a LONG time ago.

SO WHAT HAVE YOU GOT THERE, LITTLE FELLA?

POKE

I didn't think many people would show up after the whole diamond ring blow-up, but it actually seemed more crowded this year.

On top of the aunts and uncles who usually come to these things, a bunch of Mom's cousins were there, too.

Her cousin Gerald from California made the trip.
Apparently, he lived with my family for a few
months right after I was born, but I wish he
didn't have to remind me every time he sees me.

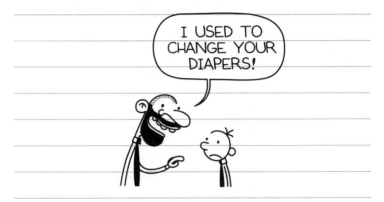

Mom's cousin Martina was there, too, and she
hasn't been to a family gathering since she struck
it rich in Las Vegas.

The way I heard it, one morning Martina was
at the hotel breakfast buffet when she noticed
another room with more food in it.

But when she made a beeline for the other room
she found out there WAS no other room.

It was actually a full-length mirror reflecting the room she was already IN.

Martina broke her collarbone and sued the hotel, so I'm pretty sure the Porsche parked in Gramma's driveway was hers.

Uncle Larry was at Gramma's, too. I don't think he's actually related to anyone, but someone invited him to a family event at some point and he's been showing up ever since.

GUESS WHO'S HERE? UNCLE LARRY!

Uncle Larry's a great guy and all, but he always parks himself in the best seat in Gramma's family room and doesn't move until it's time to leave.

Gramma's two sisters both came this year, even though they can't STAND each other. Every Christmas they exchange presents, but I think the only reason they do it is to see who can come up with the most insulting gift.

FIVE KETCHUP PACKETS

USED BAR OF DEODORANT

On Easter at Gramma's house you've basically got three choices of how to occupy yourself: you can sit in the family room and watch golf on TV with the men, go in the kitchen and talk with the women, or hang out in the basement with all the kids.

None of those options really works for me, so I always just lock myself in the bathroom until it's time to eat.

The main event at Easter is brunch. The whole family used to sit at one long table in the dining room, but now that the family's bigger it's split between grown-ups and kids. The grown-ups' table is in the dining room, and the kids' table is in the kitchen.

I'm kind of glad we changed things, because when we all used to sit together I'd always end up next to someone who was WAY more interested in my life than I was.

TELL ME EVERYTHING YOU'VE LEARNED IN SOCIAL STUDIES THIS YEAR!

Plus, when we all sat together, Mom would make me eat food I didn't like. She always wants me to try her potato salad, which I might be willing to do if it wasn't served in the same bowl she uses when one of us kids has the flu.

I don't like eating in Gramma's dining room anyway because it's WAY too formal, and I think it makes everyone act too serious.

A few years ago Peepaw had a green bean hanging from his lip for most of brunch. That was funny enough on its own, but when it fell into his glass of water I had to laugh.

I thought everyone ELSE would laugh, too, but nobody did. Dad shot me a look, and I got the feeling I should just keep my head down and go back to eating my ham.

Ever since then, whenever something funny happens during a meal in the dining room, I do everything I can to stop myself from laughing. I'll pinch my inner thigh or bite my lip real hard, but sometimes even THAT'S not enough.

One year, when Peepaw went to blow out the candles on his birthday cake, his dentures came flying out.

FWOOTHP!

I strained so hard to keep myself from laughing that I thought I might burst a blood vessel or blow out an eyeball or something.

Plus, I had JUST taken a big sip of chocolate milk, and I was trying not to let it dribble on to my plate.

I tried to think of something really sad, but all I could come up with was Sweetie in his little sweater. Then one thought led to another, and it was just too much for me to take.

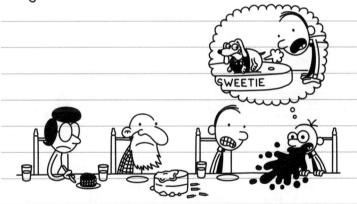

In fact, now that I think of it, that incident is probably what led to us kids having our own table in the kitchen.

I'm not sure how they figured out who qualifies as a kid and who's an adult, because Uncle Cecil sits at the grown-ups' table. I know it might SOUND like Uncle Cecil is a grown-up, but he's actually only three or four years old.

Great Aunt Marcie adopted him a few years ago, and somehow I guess that makes him my uncle. It does make things pretty awkward sometimes.

I think the rule should be that if you need a booster seat, you're automatically disqualified from sitting at the grown-ups' table. But Uncle Cecil sits in the dining room with the adults, and Rodrick has to sit at the kids' table, even though he's practically a grown man.

Today I made sure to sit as far away as I could from Malvin and Malcolm, but that meant I ended up sitting next to my second cousin, Georgia, who has a front tooth that's so loose it's hanging by a thread.

GEORGIA

Her tooth was like that the LAST time we saw her, so we're talking YEARS now. Everyone in the family tries to convince her to let them pull it out, but she's been stalling for forever.

I'M STILL FINKING ABOUT IT.

When MY front tooth was loose, I was terrified of letting someone pull it. Mom spent WEEKS trying to convince me to let her yank it out, but I was too scared. Eventually, she said if the tooth fell out in my sleep I'd swallow it and that was really dangerous.

But I knew that wasn't true, because the week before Manny had swallowed one of my toy cars and HE lived.

After a while, I guess Dad got fed up about my loose tooth and decided to take matters into his own hands. He told me he wanted to show me a magic trick, then he tied a string to my front tooth and the other end to a doorknob. I didn't see what was coming until it was too late.

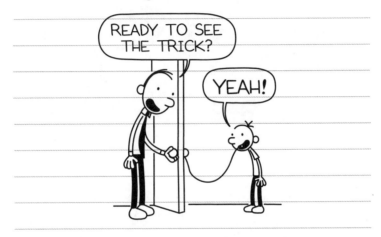

READY TO SEE THE TRICK?

YEAH!

After watching Georgia twirl her tooth in a circle with her tongue for forty-five minutes today, I went into the family room because I knew that's where Gramma keeps her string.

But when I walked in I was surprised to find that half the grown-ups were already in there, going through Gramma's photo albums.

From what I could piece together, Aunt Audra's psychic told her that Meemaw's diamond ring was in a family photo album, and when the rest of the grown-ups heard that they got all excited.

Then someone suggested that maybe the psychic didn't mean the ring was LITERALLY in a photo album, so everyone started looking through the pictures to see if there were any clues. A minute later something caught Uncle Larry's eye.

Uncle Larry was pointing at photos from the last Easter we all got together. In one picture Meemaw was wearing her diamond ring, and in the next she WASN'T.

Preparing for the
Easter egg hunt

Meemaw's famous
applesauce

It didn't take a genius to figure out where her ring went. Fifteen seconds later, everyone was fanned out across Gramma's backyard, searching for Meemaw's plastic eggs.

RUSTLE
RUSTLE

135

I guess everyone figured that if the ring was in an egg, then it was finders keepers. Mom tried to get everyone to come back inside to have dessert, but it was no use.

It was a little disturbing to see how greedy my relatives were acting, but I admit I got a little caught up in the excitement myself. While everyone else was looking for the egg OUTSIDE, I was looking for it INSIDE.

But, after Mom caught me riffling through Gramma's underwear drawer, I realized maybe I was getting a little TOO carried away.

I think Mom was pretty fed up with everyone by that point, because she told our family that we were going home.

As far as I know, nobody actually found the ring. But when we drove away from Gramma's a few people were still out there searching.

HAVE YOU LOOKED IN THAT BUSH?

<u>Tuesday</u>
Usually, when Aunt Gretchen and her kids stay
with us, it's for a week. But this time around
they only lasted two DAYS.

That's because, after what happened last night,
Dad told them they were gonna have to leave. At
dinner we'd run out of ketchup, so Malcolm had
picked up the phone and called 911 to report us.

It took about two hours for Mom and Dad to
clear everything up with the cops.

After Dad gave Aunt Gretchen and her sons the
boot, they packed up and went to Gramma's.

And I'm sure that was just fine with them,
because it meant they had more time to look for
the egg.

I was glad they left, because when they did I
got my bed back. For two nights I had to sleep
in Rodrick's room on a leaky air mattress.

No matter how much I inflated it at night, by
morning I was lying flat on the ground.

Yesterday when I woke up on Rodrick's floor,
I spotted something under his bed when I was
getting dressed.

It was one of those Magic 8 Balls. I think Rodrick got it as a present one year and must've forgotten all about it after it rolled under his bed.

I was pretty excited to find it, because I've never got to play around with one of those things before.

The way you use the Magic 8 Ball is by asking it a question, then shaking it and waiting for your answer to appear in a little window at the back.

I was curious to see if it actually WORKED, so I gave it a try. I thought up a question and concentrated real hard, then gave the Magic 8 Ball a good shake.

A few seconds later, this is what showed up in the little window –

I have to say, I was pretty impressed. But I needed to ask this thing a few more questions to make sure it was for real.

DON'T YOU THINK ROWLEY AND ABIGAIL ARE TOTALLY OBNOXIOUS?

And every single time it was right on the money.

Even when I tried to throw it for a loop, I got an answer that seemed pretty reasonable.

Then I realized this thing wasn't only good for answering QUESTIONS. I could ask it for ADVICE, too.

I started by asking the Magic 8 Ball if I should take a shower and if I really needed to finish the outline for my Science Fair project. I got a "Yes" on the hygiene issue, but the Magic 8 Ball totally let me off the hook on my project.

MY SOURCES SAY NO

See, THIS is what's been missing my whole life. Now that I've got something to help me make all the LITTLE decisions, I'm free to focus on the IMPORTANT stuff.

In school we learned that Albert Einstein wore the same clothes every day so he didn't have to waste any brainpower on deciding what to wear.

And that's exactly what THIS thing's gonna do for me.

In fact, after using the Magic 8 Ball for just one day, I don't know how I ever got by WITHOUT it.

## Thursday

After playing around with the Magic 8 Ball for a few days, I found out it has some limitations. But that doesn't mean I'm gonna give up on it just YET. I tried using it to help me with my maths homework a few times, but it turns out it's not so good at giving you specific answers.

IF X-43=19, WHAT'S THE VALUE OF X?

WITHOUT A DOUBT

Plus, sometimes when you REALLY need an answer from the Magic 8 Ball, it can totally leave you hanging.

Today on my way home from school, one of the Mingo kids came after me with a stick. I asked the Magic 8 Ball if I should run away or fight, and gave it a hard shake.

For some reason, the Magic 8 Ball couldn't make up its mind.

But the Magic 8 Ball TOTALLY made up for it later on in the day. Mom told me I've been spending too much time indoors and that I needed to go outside and get some fresh air.

When Mom left the room I asked the Magic 8 Ball if I should take her advice, and its answer could not have been more clear.

So I hid in Mom's closet, which I knew would be the LAST place she'd come looking for me.

While I was waiting Mom out in there, I noticed a bunch of books on the top shelf.

They were hidden behind some shoe boxes, so it was pretty clear Mom didn't want anyone to find them. At first I couldn't figure out why she was keeping all these books tucked away in her closet instead of on a shelf out in the open. But when I read the titles I totally got it.

These books are basically Mom's secret weapon, and she doesn't want us kids to KNOW about them.

I flipped through a few of the books, and some were really eye-opening. I found one that was about using something called "reverse psychology".

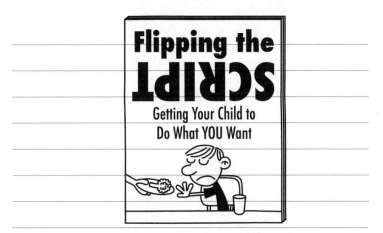

The idea is that you can get your kids to do what you want by telling them to do the OPPOSITE. Now that I think of it, Mom and Dad have been using that technique on us ever since I can remember.

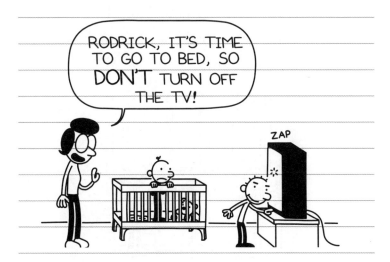

When I was little, I used to BEG Mom and Dad to let me do the dishes, but they'd always tell me I was too young to help out.

Finally, on my eighth birthday they let me dry the dishes, and I was so happy they might as well have given me a million dollars. Now I realize the whole thing was a trick, and Rodrick must've fallen into the same trap.

There were books for just about every type of
situation a parent might have to deal with while
raising their kids. I've always wondered where
Mom gets all her advice, and now I know.

When I was nine I found an inchworm crawling up
our front steps, and I named him Squirm and kept
him in a little jar with holes poked in the top.

Every day I'd let him out of the jar so he could
get some exercise.

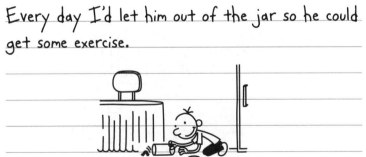

This was just about the time Manny was starting to take his first steps, which was unfortunate for Squirm the worm.

I was really torn up about it, and that night Mom came into my room to talk.

She told me I shouldn't be sad, because Squirm was in "Inchworm Heaven" and that in Inchworm Heaven it's always sunny and there are tons of leaves to eat. And I've gotta admit that DID make me feel better about things.

Well, today I found the EXACT place where Mom got that idea.

One of the books on Mom's shelf looked pretty new, and when I pulled it down a LOT of things started to make sense.

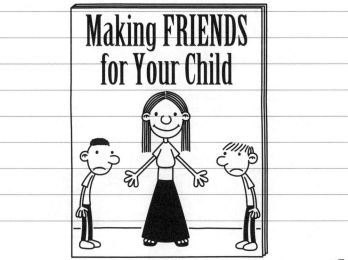

Mom's closet answered some other mysteries, too. When I was in kindergarten I had a stuffed animal called Tickles that I slept with every single night.

That summer we went away on holiday to the beach, and I took Tickles with me. But one afternoon when we came back to our hotel room Tickles was GONE.

Mom said the cleaning lady must've scooped up Tickles when she took the sheets, so we went down to the place where they do the laundry to see if he was in the washer or something.

But he wasn't THERE, either. By this time I was pretty hysterical, so Mom told me I should make some signs, which we put up all over the hotel.

# HAVE YOU SEEN ME?

**NAME:** TICKLES

**SIZE:** 15 INCHES

**LAST SEEN:**
OCEAN VIEW MOTEL

**RETURN TO:**
OCEAN VIEW MOTEL
FRONT DESK

The next day we went to the beach, but I couldn't enjoy myself because of Tickles.

Dad played one of those carnival games and won me a stuffed animal to replace Tickles, but it wasn't the same.

Losing Tickles pretty much ruined the holiday for EVERYONE, so we left for home a day early. I went to sleep when we got back that night, and the next morning Tickles was sitting on top of my dresser.

Mom said Tickles must've found his way home because he loved me so much. And that's what I believed for a long time.

But, hidden away behind Mom's books, there were FIVE stuffed monkeys that looked EXACTLY like Tickles.

So that means Mom must've gone out and bought a bunch of replacement monkeys right after I lost the original.

Who even KNOWS which version of Tickles is sitting on the shelf in my closet right now.

In fact, now that I think about it, I remember a time when Mom had to wash Tickles because I'd spilled some chocolate milk on him. When she opened the washing machine door, it looked like a pillow had exploded in there.

But that night after my bath Tickles was back on my bed, good as new. So the one in my room could be a fourth or fifth generation for all I know.

This ALSO explains why Manny sleeps with ten stuffed dinosaurs every night.

He used to only have ONE dinosaur he called Rexy, but Manny must've discovered Mom's hidden stash of back-ups WAY before I did.

I wanted to keep exploring Mom's closet to see what ELSE I could find, but I heard Mom coming upstairs, so I had to slip out of there.

Now that I know about Mom's parenting books, I should be able to keep one step ahead of my folks. And I can thank the Magic 8 Ball for THAT.

Tuesday
Tonight I decided to see if any of the tricks in Mom's books would actually work on ADULTS.

I've been asking Mom and Dad for my own phone for FOREVER, but Mom always says I already HAVE one. She's talking about my Ladybug phone, though, and that's more like a pre-school toy.

So when me and Rodrick were doing the dishes tonight I took a crack at using reverse psychology on Mom and Dad.

I DON'T ACTUALLY WANT MY OWN PHONE, BECAUSE IT'S TOO MUCH RESPONSIBILITY.

I didn't know what to expect, but I was shocked to see how FAST it worked. Right after that, Mom came into my room and told me she'd decided to upgrade her phone and was giving her USED one to ME.

But before she handed it over, she said there were some "ground rules". She said I had to share the phone with Manny because he uses it to play educational games.

She also said I'm not allowed to text any of my friends with it.

Well, texting my friends isn't gonna be a problem, because at the moment I don't HAVE any. Sharing with Manny is another issue.

Manny likes to take pictures on Mom's phone, but I really don't need HIS pictures mixed in with MINE.

FLASH

Still, I was pretty excited to get my hands on a decent phone.

I spent some time personalizing it with a new wallpaper and different ringtones. But, in the middle of doing that, I got a text from Gramma that was obviously meant for Mom.

**Texting with
Mom**

**Can Frank come by this weekend with the boys and move the piano to the basement?**

Mom said I wasn't allowed to text my friends, but she never said anything about RELATIVES.

**Sorry they are doing father/son stuff this wknd.**

After that was taken care of, I downloaded a bunch of games and started having some fun.

But, right in the middle of a game, Aunt Veronica called on video chat.

The LAST thing I expected to see in the privacy of my bathroom was Aunt Veronica's FACE.

So I think I can be excused for being a little surprised.

I fished the phone out of the toilet and did everything I could to get it to turn on, but it was no use.

I feel kind of bad for ruining it, but, in my defence, I DID try to warn Mom and Dad I wasn't ready for that kind of responsibility.

165

<u>Wednesday</u>

I've been getting tired of having to fear for my life whenever I walk by the Mingo kids' woods, but I realized those guys only really pick on the after-school crowd. So I decided my smartest move was to just wait them out.

That meant I needed to find something to kill time once school ended. There are a whole bunch of clubs for students, but I've never really been that interested until now.

Maths Club

Drama Club

International Relations Club

Poetry Club

Today I stayed after school to see if there was something that would be a good fit.

The Board Game Club sounded like it might be pretty fun, but it's run by Mr Nern, and I've already spent enough time with him for one school year.

There's a Pillow-Fighting Club, too, but one look inside the room where they meet told me it wasn't really my thing.

There are some clubs that are REALLY on the fringe, like the Free Hugs Club that just started up this spring.

It was too hard to decide what to do, so I left it up to the Magic 8 Ball. I walked to each door where the different clubs meet and gave the 8 Ball a shake to see which one I should join.

I got a lot of "No"s and a few "Ask Again Later"s, but I finally got a "Yes, Definitely" when I was in front of the Yearbook Club door.

I walked inside, and the staff looked like it was in the middle of a meeting.

I waited at the back until the meeting broke up, then went to the editor-in-chief, Betsy Buckles, and asked if I could join.

She said the yearbook was almost finished, but they needed a few more photos for the "Candids" page. Then she said the school would pay five bucks for every photo that ended up in the yearbook, and I was sold.

If I can avoid the Mingo kids AND get paid, that's a win-win.

<u>Thursday</u>
Today was my first day as the yearbook
photographer, and it wasn't as easy as I
thought it would be. I wanted to get good
pictures, but, to be honest, kids at my school
don't really do anything that INTERESTING.

I was trying to do my job taking pictures while
ALSO being a full-time student, and that didn't
make things any easier.

I was hoping somebody would do something really dumb and I'd get a great picture of it. But for some reason people were on their best behaviour today. One shot I was DYING to get was Jamar Law with his head stuck in a chair.

There was a picture of him doing that in the LAST yearbook, and if he did it again I wanted to be ready for it. I know a photographer isn't supposed to influence his subjects, but I tried to at LEAST nudge Jamar in the right direction.

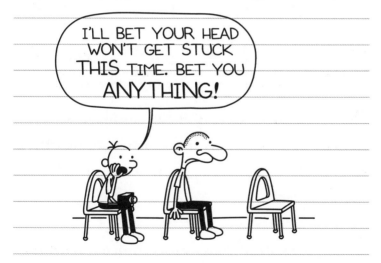

I'LL BET YOUR HEAD WON'T GET STUCK THIS TIME. BET YOU ANYTHING!

Whenever I see a picture in a yearbook or a magazine, there's always a little caption underneath.

So when I turned in my photos at the end of the day, I wrote little blurbs so Betsy would know what she was looking at.

*I'm pretty sure Doug Parker's fly is open here.*

*Morons on the bus.*

*Trevor Wilson leaves the bathroom without washing his hands.*

*Not again! Chad Middleton goes to the nurse's office with a bloody nose.*

The great thing about pictures nowadays is that everything is digital, so if you don't like something about a photo you took you can always tweak it on the computer.

I took a couple of shots at lunch where somebody blinked, and those photos would've been USELESS if I hadn't been able to edit them.

I figure every yearbook needs a little humour, so I edited a few pictures to make them funnier. Hopefully, Mr Blakely won't be too mad when he sees his.

I realized being the yearbook photographer gives me a lot of POWER, too.

I can decide who gets in the yearbook and who DOESN'T. And, if there's somebody who ANNOYS me, I can get some revenge.

I took a picture of Leon Feast after school, and when I played around with it on the computer I shrunk his head by 75%. I seriously hope that one gets past the editors. And if it does I give all credit to the Magic 8 Ball.

Monday
Over the weekend I got a chance to go back into Mom's closet, and I found my old Body Blankie behind her winter boots.

I couldn't BELIEVE it. I'd been looking for that thing for the past few months, and it was in Mom's closet all along.

I got the Body Blankie as a Christmas gift last year from Mom and Dad. When I looked at the box, I have to admit I wasn't too thrilled about it.

That changed the minute I put it on. Let me just say for the record that whoever invented the Body Blankie is a GENIUS.

You know when you're watching TV with a blanket wrapped round you and you want to grab your drink or the remote control, so you have to take the whole thing off to free up your hands?

Well, the Body Blankie SOLVES all that. It's like a regular blanket, but with sleeves that have MITTENS at the ends. So you can grab stuff without ever exposing your skin to the cold air.

The Body Blankie is made of flannel, so having it on is like being in bed all the time.

RODRICK got a Body Blankie, too, and I think he liked HIS even more than I liked MINE. In fact, after Rodrick put his on for the first time, he didn't take it off for something like five days.

I think he would've stayed in it for good if Mom hadn't made him take a shower.

Rodrick used to only sleep in his bed or on the couch, but once he had his Body Blankie he pretty much dozed off whenever the mood struck him.

Mom and Dad put up with it for a little while, but me and Rodrick probably took it too far, and our Body Blankies mysteriously disappeared soon after that.

When I found my Body Blankie this weekend, I didn't know what to DO.

If I started parading around the house in it, Mom would know I've been poking around in her closet. The only place I could really wear it was in bed, but that seemed to kind of defeat the purpose.

But this morning when I was getting ready for school I got an idea.

I realized if I put my Body Blankie on UNDER my school clothes no one would even know. And being in class would be like being in BED.

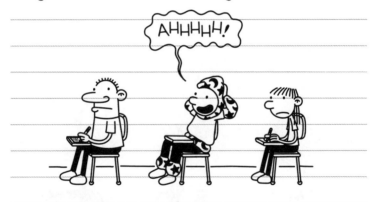

But I wish I'd thought it through a little better. The Body Blankie might be comfortable to wear while watching TV at home, but walking to SCHOOL in it was a whole other matter.

The leggings of the Body Blankie are really short, so you look like a penguin when you walk.

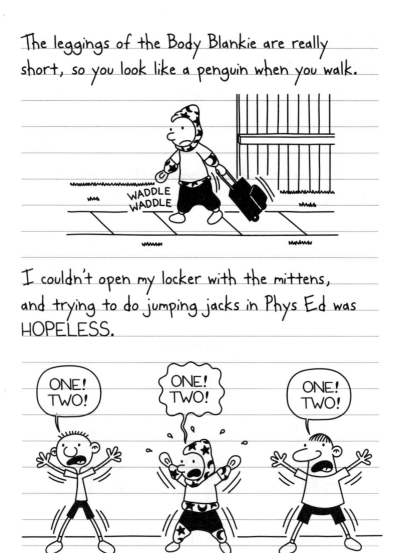

I couldn't open my locker with the mittens, and trying to do jumping jacks in Phys Ed was HOPELESS.

Plus, I found out the disadvantage of flannel is that it gets really HOT.

After Phys Ed, the Body Blankie footies were filled with sweat, and I knew it was time to bail on the idea.

But, when I tried to take the Body Blankie OFF, the zipper snapped.

I should've KNOWN never to trust a product that's advertised on TV.

I tried to wriggle out of it by pushing my arms up through the hole where my head was, but I couldn't get my elbows out.

I started to go into a panic because there was no ventilation in that thing, and I was worried I was gonna get baked alive like a microwave burrito.

After a minute I took a lot of deep breaths to calm myself down. At that point there were only a few more classes to go, and then I could cut myself free at home.

My last class was Social Studies, and we had a test. I wasn't prepared at ALL, so I was glad when I found out it was true/false.

Because that's EXACTLY the kind of thing the Magic 8 Ball is good at.

When the test started I pulled the Magic 8 Ball out of my bag and went through the questions one by one. A few of the answers didn't look right to me, but the Magic 8 Ball had got me THIS far and I wasn't gonna start questioning it now.

It was STILL pretty time-consuming, though. Kids were handing in their tests, and I wasn't even halfway through yet.

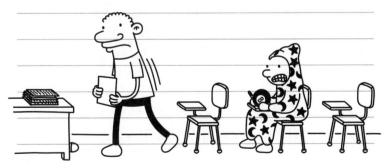

I started getting nervous that I wasn't gonna finish before the bell rang, and the Magic 8 Ball was doing some SERIOUS stalling.

I shook it faster to try to get real answers, and that's when I lost a handle on it.

The Magic 8 Ball hit the ground hard and, before I could grab it, it rolled RIGHT to Mrs Merritt.

Just then the bell rang and, after the class was let out, Mrs Merritt took me down to Vice Principal Roy's office. Mrs Merritt told him she had caught me red-handed using a "high-tech cheating device" on my test.

I think Vice Principal Roy was a little confused, but he took Mrs Merritt's complaint seriously anyway. He called MOM, and ten minutes later she was in his office.

I've got to give Mom credit, because she stuck up for me. She said the Magic 8 Ball was just a "harmless toy" and that I COULDN'T have been using it to cheat.

I wanted to interrupt Mom and tell her not to disrespect the Magic 8 Ball by calling it a toy, but I figured that could wait until later. Plus, Mom hadn't said anything about the Body Blankie yet and I didn't want to risk making her mad.

I thought Vice Principal Roy was gonna let me off the hook, but then he pulled up my record on his computer. He said my grades have been going downhill lately and that I'm slipping in every subject. Then he said I haven't turned in a homework assignment for three weeks.

Well, that might be true, but ever since Fregley ditched my textbooks it's been a little hard for me to do my assignments.

Then Vice Principal Roy totally dropped a bomb on me. He said that if I didn't improve my grades in the next few weeks I was gonna have to go to SUMMER school.

THAT got my attention. I've heard rumours about summer school, and it's not something I really want to be a part of.

For one thing, I know they shut off the air-conditioning during the summer to save money.

The classes are more like detention than school, and none of the regular teachers are there. In fact, I heard the English teacher for summer school is the JANITOR.

I don't know if Vice Principal Roy was just trying to scare me, but, if he was, it WORKED. Because the thought of spending my summer holiday with Mr Meeks is enough to turn me into a straight-A student.

Thursday

I'm not really sure how my grades got so bad, because my year actually started off pretty GOOD. In the first quarter I got As and Bs on my report card, and Mom even took me out to get a hot-fudge sundae to celebrate my accomplishment.

RODRICK got in on the action, too, even though his report card that quarter was lousy.

That taught me that even if you try your best someone's just gonna mooch off your hard work.

I know I'm not the best student or anything, but I've never had to worry about going to SUMMER school.

So this week I've been doing everything I can to get my situation under control. Mom got me a set of used textbooks, and I've been catching up on my assignments every night.

But some of the classes I'm flunking don't even HAVE homework. One is Music, and my problem THERE is that I don't participate. None of the boys really do, which is why Mrs Norton comes right up in our faces and tries to get us to sing.

If Mr Meeks is the ENGLISH teacher in summer school, then I don't even wanna imagine what Music class looks like.

I decided that, starting TODAY, I was gonna be Mrs Norton's best student.

So, when she called my name at the start of class, I stood right up and belted out the song we've been working on.

THERE'S A **HOLE** IN THE BUCKET, ♪ ♫ DEAR LIZA, DEAR LIZA! ♪ ♫ THERE'S A **HOLE** IN THE BUCKET, ♪ ♫ DEAR LIZA, A HOLE! ♪ ♫

Mrs Norton waited until I was finished, then she said she wasn't asking me to SING, she was just calling attendance.

All week, Mom's been helping me catch up on my missing homework assignments, but the one thing she says I'm gonna have to do on my OWN is the Science Fair project. And that kind of stinks, because Science isn't exactly my strong suit.

For LAST year's Science Fair, my experiment was on metamorphosis. I collected a dozen or so caterpillars and put them in a box with leaves to eat, and they all made cocoons.

My plan was to open the box at the EXACT moment they turned into butterflies and blow the judges away.

I worked hard on it, and even turned in my project a day EARLY. But I left the box with the caterpillars on the heater in the Science classroom, and unfortunately that was the end of that.

Today during recess I was in the library trying to get ideas for my Science Fair project, and Betsy Buckles came in to say they needed me in the yearbook office.

She said the Class Favourites results were in, and she asked me to take pictures of the winners.

I didn't bother to vote this year, so I wasn't even sure who was on the ballot. But, once the winners started filing in through the door, it wasn't too hard to figure out who had won what.

MOST LIKELY TO SUCCEED

MOST ATHLETIC

MOST FRIENDLY

BEST SMILE

Most of the winners were exactly who you'd expect. Bryce Anderson won Best Hair, Cecilia Faramir won Most Talented, and Jenna Stewart won Best Dressed.

The only REAL surprise was Liam Nelson, who won Best Looking. But Liam works on the yearbook staff and was in charge of counting up the votes, so something tells me he fudged the results.

When Fregley walked through the door, I got confused. The only category I could see him winning was Class Clown, but I had just finished taking Jeffrey Laffley's picture.

So I looked over the list Betsy gave me and found out Fregley had been voted MOST POPULAR. But the way things have been going lately, I guess I shouldn't have been surprised.

I was already in a pretty bad mood when the last two people walked in the room to have their picture taken.

I looked down at the printout and, when I scanned all the way to the bottom, I felt sick.

| Cutest Couple | Rowley Jefferson + Abigail Brown |
|---|---|

I've had to do some unpleasant things in my life, but, believe me, NOTHING compares to what I had to suffer through today.

After that I officially resigned as yearbook photographer and turned in my camera. Because, really, there's only so much one person can take.

<u>Monday</u>

Things have really fallen apart for me ever since I dropped my Magic 8 Ball in Mrs Merritt's class.

After Vice Principal Roy gave it back to me, I noticed it seemed a lot lighter. It turned out that when it hit the floor it had cracked and the blue liquid behind the little window had leaked out. So that meant it was totally USELESS.

RATTLE
RATTLE

I ended up tossing it over Gramma's fence on the way home from school that day. But lately I've missed having it, because I've had some REALLY tricky decisions to make.

I finally caught up on my missing homework assignments, but my Science Fair project is due on Thursday, and I still don't even have an IDEA for it yet.

So I thought of Erick Glick. I've always heard he could hook you up with an old assignment if you were in a pinch, and I figured maybe he could even get his hands on a Science Fair project.

But, still, I didn't know if I wanted to get involved with a shady character like Erick. This was just the kind of decision I'd ordinarily leave up to the Magic 8 Ball, but today I was totally on my own.

I was pretty desperate, though, so at recess I found Erick hanging out behind the school and told him about my situation.

Erick said he could take care of me. He did some kind of secret knock on a door a few feet away that had no handle on it. Then the door opened from the inside.

It took a minute for my eyes to adjust to the darkness. The room was apparently some kind of storage area, and there were half a dozen kids crowded round a desk with a pile of papers on it.

There were old book reports and history papers, and a bunch of other stuff, too.

The person who seemed to be in charge was Dennis Denard, who's in eighth grade but got held back twice. I'm guessing he stayed in middle school on PURPOSE because he's got such a good racket going on.

Erick told Dennis I needed a Science Fair project, and he took me to a separate area in the back where there were SHELVES of old ones.

As far as I could tell, the better the project, the more it cost.

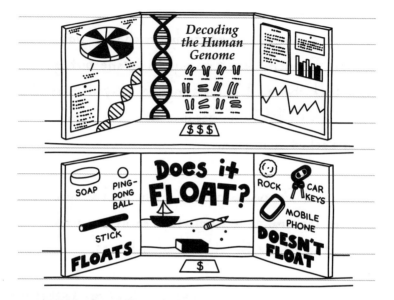

One of the projects seemed kind of familiar, and when I took a closer look I knew why. It was RODRICK'S Science Fair project from when HE was in middle school.

I remember Rodrick working on that one. His idea was to see if different types of music have an effect on how fast flowers grow.

So he put a potted flower in every place in the
house where there was music.

The flowers all died within two weeks, and Rodrick
thought the music killed them. But Mom told him
the reason the plants died was because he never
WATERED them.

I guess the school just dumps all the old Science Fair projects in the storage room, whether they got a decent grade or not.

I don't know if seeing Rodrick's old project is what did it, but I started having second thoughts about this whole thing. I think Dennis and Erick could tell I was getting cold feet, because they pressured me to make a decision.

I told Dennis I didn't have any money on me and that I'd come back tomorrow.

Erick told me to turn my pockets inside out to PROVE it, but I noticed the door to the outside was open a crack and I bolted.

I'm not sure I'm ready to get involved with the Dennis Denards and Erick Glicks of the world anyway. Because once you take that first step there's no turning back.

<u>Wednesday</u>

Well, I didn't see THIS coming. One week after Rowley and Abigail got voted Cutest Couple, word on the playground is that they're through.

I heard that Abigail is back with her old boyfriend, Michael Sampson, and people are saying the only reason she got together with Rowley in the first place was to make Michael jealous.

Apparently, it WORKED. But, from what I heard, the way Rowley found out was kind of harsh.

SLURP
SMACK

But I can't spend a lot of time feeling sorry for Rowley, because I've got problems of my OWN.

Yesterday I had to stay after school for the second day in a row doing research for my Science Fair project, which is due tomorrow.

And, by the way, I'm glad I decided not to go the Dennis Denard route, because today somebody tipped off a teacher and a bunch of the faculty members staged a raid on the storage room.

207

The kids who got caught were given detention for the rest of the year, and I'm sure the punishment includes an automatic trip to summer school.

I've still got a chance to get OUT of summer school, and I really hope I DO, because I don't want to be staring at Dennis Denard's sweaty back for the rest of the summer.

Thursday
I worked on my Science Fair project yesterday from the time I got home until 11:30 at night. I wouldn't say my project is gonna win the Nobel Prize or anything, but I was proud of myself for actually getting it DONE.

I think Mom was pretty happy, too. But after I was finished she went over the requirements that Mrs Abbington sent home, and it said in big bold letters that the written report had to be TYPED.

Mom said there was no use complaining and that I needed to get started on typing up the report.

But I had already spent all my energy getting to THAT point, so I told Mom I was gonna go to sleep and wake up extra early to get the work done.

I set my alarm for 6:00, but when I woke up this morning it was 8:10. I totally freaked out because I didn't remember hitting the snooze bar even ONCE.

I knew I was in trouble because I had to leave for school in twenty minutes and there was no WAY I could type it up before then.

But when I went downstairs my Science Fair project was sitting on the kitchen table, and the whole thing was TYPED.

For a second I thought maybe the Science Report Fairy had come in overnight and sprinkled some pixie dust on the pages, but then I realized it was MOM.

I went up to her room to thank her, but she was out cold.

I handed in my Science Fair project during second period, and I felt like a HUGE weight had been lifted off my shoulders. For the rest of the day, I actually ENJOYED myself at school.

Rowley, on the other hand, was not doing so good.

At recess he just wandered around with a dazed look on his face, and once or twice I saw him near the Find a Friend station.

I thought about going over and talking to him, but Mr Nern beat me to it.

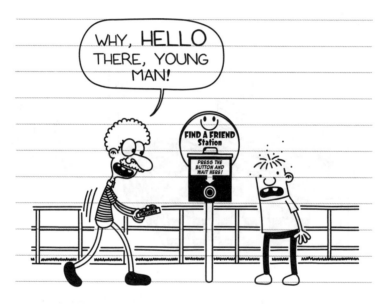

WHY, HELLO THERE, YOUNG MAN!

FIND A FRIEND
Station

PRESS THE
BUTTON AND
WAIT HERE!

The more I thought about it, the more I realized me and Rowley are probably better off not being friends anyway. We've been going back and forth for so long that enough is enough already.

But seeing Rowley play checkers on the bench with Mr Nern made me feel really guilty.

I couldn't decide what to do about Rowley, so I went to the one place where I knew I could get an answer.

On the way home from school, I stopped by Gramma's house to see if I could find the Magic 8 Ball in her backyard. I knew it was broken, but I thought somehow I could get one more good answer out of it.

It took a long time, but I finally found it near the woodpile.

I was ready to concentrate real hard and ask my question, but that's when I noticed something green and shiny poking out from under a log.

I forgot all about the Magic 8 Ball and went for the plastic egg.

I gave it a little shake, and when I heard the sound it made I knew EXACTLY what was inside.

RATTLE
RATTLE

I couldn't believe the Magic 8 Ball had led me directly to Meemaw's diamond ring. It probably figured it OWED me one for everything that's happened recently.

Once I knew I had Meemaw's ring, a MILLION thoughts went through my head, and most of them involved a jet pack.

But I remembered what Mom said would happen if someone actually FOUND the ring. And, even though I could probably sell it for good money, it's not worth breaking up the family over it.

So I took the egg and hid it where nobody will find it, or at least not for a while. But if I'm ever hard up for cash I know I can always go to the spot between Tickles four and five to get out of a jam.

Monday

The Magic 8 Ball might be good for helping out with the little decisions, but I figure the BIG ones are up to me.

So at lunch today I went to the back of the line where Rowley was sitting and asked him if he wanted to come sit with ME. And five seconds later it was just like old times.

I know Mom's always saying friends come and go and family is forever, and maybe that's true.

But your family isn't gonna be there when Meckley Mingo chases you with his belt on your way home from school.

I'm sure me and Rowley will get in another fight somewhere down the road and then we'll go through this drama all over again. But for now we're good.

Or at least until the YEARBOOK comes out. But I figure we can always deal with THAT later on.

*Cutest Couple*
Rowley & Abigail

## ACKNOWLEDGEMENTS

Thanks to all the terrific Wimpy Kid fans around the world who make writing these books so rewarding. Thank you for inspiring and energizing me.

Thanks to my family for years of support and love. I feel very blessed to be a part of your lives.

Thanks to everyone at Abrams for turning me into a published author and for taking such care to create great books. Thanks to my editor, Charlie Kochman, for your dedication and passion. Thanks to Michael Jacobs for helping Greg Heffley reach ever higher heights. Thanks to Jason Wells, Veronica Wasserman, Scott Auerbach, Jen Graham, Chad W. Beckerman and Susan Van Metre for your work and for your friendship.

Thanks to everyone at Poptropica, especially Jess Brallier, for your belief that kids deserve great storytelling.

Thanks to Sylvie Rabineau, my wonderful agent, for your guidance. Thanks to Brad Simpson and Nina Jacobson for bringing Greg Heffley to life on the silver screen, and thanks to Roland Poindexter, Ralph Millero and Vanessa Morrison for helping bring Greg Heffley to life in a new way.

Thanks to Shaelyn Germain and Anna Cesary for working with me through the madness of multiple endeavours.

## ABOUT THE AUTHOR

Jeff Kinney is an online game developer and designer, and a #1 *New York Times* bestselling author. Jeff has been named one of *Time* magazine's 100 Most Influential People in the World. Jeff is also the creator of *Poptropica.com*, which was named one of *Time* magazine's 50 Best Websites. He spent his childhood in the Washington, D.C., area and moved to New England in 1995. Jeff lives in southern Massachusetts with his wife and their two sons.

Ever wanted to be just as POPULAR as Greg?

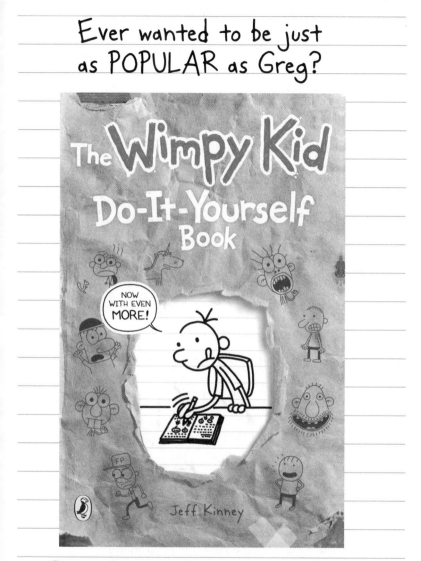

Record your funniest moments for future generations!

# Predict the

Robots and mankind will be locked in a battle for supremacy.   TRUE ☐   FALSE ☐

Parents will be banned from dancing within twenty feet of their children.   TRUE ☐   FALSE ☐

People will have instant-messaging chips implanted in their brains.   TRUE ☐   FALSE ☐

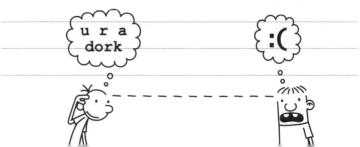

# FUTURE

YOUR FIVE BOLD PREDICTIONS FOR THE FUTURE:

**1.**

**2.**

**3.**

**4.**

**5.**

(WRITE EVERYTHING DOWN NOW
SO YOU CAN TELL YOUR FRIENDS
"I TOLD YOU SO" LATER ON.)

# Predict YOUR

Answer these questions, then check back when you're an adult to see how you did!

## WHEN I'M THIRTY YEARS OLD

I will live _____ kilometres from my current home.

I will be:  MARRIED ☐   SINGLE ☐

I will have _____ kids and a _____ named _____.

I will work as a _____ and make _____ dollars a year.

I will live in a _____ on a _____.

I will take a _____ to work every day.

# future

I will be ____ metres ____ centimetres tall.

I will have the same basic haircut
I have now. TRUE ☐  FALSE ☐

I will have the same best friend I have right
now. TRUE ☐  FALSE ☐

I will be in really
excellent shape.
TRUE ☐  FALSE ☐

I will listen to the same kind of music I listen to
now. TRUE ☐  FALSE ☐

I will have visited ____ different countries.

The thing that will change the most about me
between now and then will be: _____
_____
_____ .

# Predict YOUR

What you're basically gonna do here is roll a dice over and over, crossing off items when you land on them, like this:

**1ST ROLL:** 🎲

HOME:
1 Apartment
2 House
3 ~~Mansion~~

**2ND ROLL:** 🎲
1 Igloo

2

LOCATION:
1 ~~Mountains~~
2 Beach
3 City

**3RD ROLL:** 🎲
~~Iceberg~~

Keep going through the list, and when you get to the end, jump back to the beginning. When there's only one item left in a category, circle it. Once you've got an item in each category circled, you'll know your future! Good luck!

# future

HOME:
- Apartment
- House
- Mansion
- Igloo

LOCATION:
- Mountains
- Beach
- City
- Iceberg

KIDS:
- None
- One
- Two
- Ten

PET:
- Dog
- Cat
- Bird
- Turtle

JOB:
- Doctor
- Actor
- Clown
- Mechanic
- Lawyer
- Pilot
- Pro athlete
- Dentist
- Magician
- Whatever you want

VEHICLE:
- Car
- Motorcycle
- Helicopter
- Skateboard

SALARY:
- $100 a year
- $100,000 a year
- $1 million a year
- $100 million a year

# Things you should do

☐ Stay up all night.

☐ Ride on a roller coaster with a loop in it.

☐ Get in a food fight. THWAP

☐ Get an autograph from a famous person.

☐ Get a hole-in-one in miniature golf.

☐ Give yourself a haircut.

☐ Write down an idea for an invention.

☐ Spend three nights in a row away from home.

☐ Mail someone a letter with a real stamp and everything.

Dear Gramma, Please send money.

I ONLY HAVE A FEW MORE TO GO!

# before you get old

☐ Go on a campout.

☐ Read a whole book with no pictures in it.

☐ Beat someone who's older than you in a footrace.

☐ Make it through a whole lollipop without biting it.

☐ Use a porta-potty.

KNOCK KNOCK

OCCUPIED!

☐ Score at least one point in an organized sport.

☐ Try out for a talent show.

EH?

# How well do you

Answer these questions, and then ask your friend the same things. Keep track of how many answers you got right.

FRIEND'S NAME: _____

Has your friend ever been carsick? _____

If your friend could meet any celebrity, who would it be? _____

Where was your friend born? _____

Has your friend ever laughed so hard that milk came out of their nose? _____

Has your friend ever been sent to the principal's office? _____

9–10: YOU KNOW YOUR FRIEND SO WELL IT'S SCARY
6–8: NOT BAD...YOU KNOW YOUR FRIEND PRETTY WELL!

# know your FRIEND?

What's your friend's favourite
junk food? _____

Has your friend ever broken
a bone? _____

When was the last time your
friend wet the bed? _____

If your friend had to
permanently transform into
an animal, what animal would
it be? _____

Is your friend secretly
afraid of clowns? _____

Now count up your correct answers and look at the
scale below to see how you did.

2–5: DID YOU GUYS JUST MEET OR SOMETHING?
0–1: TIME TO GET A NEW FRIEND

# Take a friendship

Want to see if you and your friend are a good match? First, go through each pair of items below and circle the one you like best.

# COMPATIBILITY TEST

Then have your friend go through the same list and make their selections. See how well your answers match up!

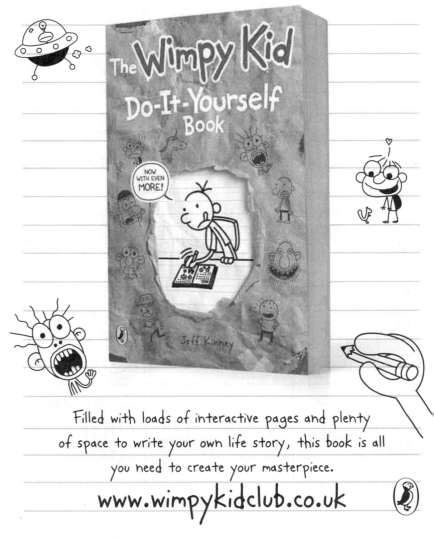

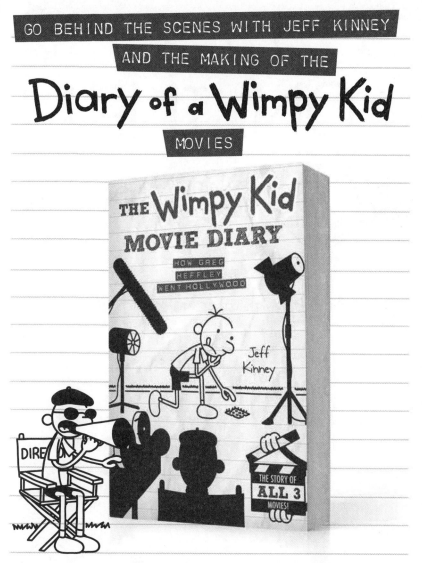

# GET ONLINE!

Join
www.wimpykidclub.co.uk

- Hang out with other **Wimpy Kid** fans
  - Don't be a loser - get the
    latest news first
  - Are you a wimp or a moron?
Battle it out on Wimp Wars to win Mom Bucks
  - Read sneak previews of all the
    Wimpy Kid books
  - Test your Wimpy Kid knowledge

TYPE
TYPE